This igloo book belongs to:

_____

igloobooks

Published in 2014
by Igloo Books Ltd
Cottage Farm
Sywell
NN6 0BJ
www.igloobooks.com

HUN001 1114
2 4 6 8 10 9 7 5 3 1
ISBN 978-1-78343-653-8

Written by Elizabeth Dale
Illustrated by Becka Moore

Printed and manufactured in China

His Royal Shyness

Elizabeth Dale

Becka Moor

igloobooks

Prince Bertie was a royal and a handsome, little lad.
The king and queen would show him off at any chance they had.

The townsfolk all cheered loudly when the royal prince rode by, but Bertie, to the town's surprise, was very, very...

... shy!

"Please come and shake a hand or two,"
his loving mum would coo.
"Or meet the marching band," said Dad.
"They can't wait to meet YOU!"

Young Bertie stared, a little SCARED,
then ran behind his throne.
He sucked his little, royal thumb
until they all went home.

The queen said, "Bertie, you're just shy," and gently squeezed his hand.

"Don't worry, we'll find help for you. We'll search throughout the land."

So, doctors came from far and wide, each one was very sure,
that they alone had got the only anti-shyness cure.

The doctors all looked really odd, they said,
"We'll help you, sire!"
Poor Bertie was so scared of them,
he trembled and grew shyer!

An old magician smiled and said,
"I'll cure him with a spell."
Poor Bertie still felt shy and now
he was dizzy as well.

"My Courage Cake will make him brave!" declared the palace cook.

So, Bertie ate a chunk and found... his hands no longer shook.

He smiled and cut a huge, big piece and ate it all so fast.

"I really think," declared the king,
"that Bertie's cured at last!"

"We'll hold a garden party," said the queen. "I cannot wait. Our guests will come from near and far to help us celebrate!"

The trumpets **blew,** the guests arrived, the sun shone high and bright. Bertie smiled at everyone, **then ...**

... scurried out of sight!
From underneath the table, Bertie shook from head to toe.

Then suddenly, his gran
appeared and said,
"Don't worry so."

She hugged the prince and said,
"I used to **hide** beneath here, too.

When I was a small princess,
I was **just** as scared as you."

"The answer is to find some **fun** in everything you see. For **laughter** is the cure," said Gran. "I'm sure you will agree!"

When people seem too **scary**, all you ever need to do, is play some silly games and make them laugh along with you.

Then, Bertie told some **funny** jokes and did a silly dance.

He **cartwheeled** all around the pond...

... and made his pony **prance.**

The duchesses joined in the fun and cried out, "We want more!"
So, Bertie quickly organised a crazy tug of war.

"Everyone fell over, but they'd had the best fun ever.
"Thank you, Gran," said Bertie. "You're really very clever."

So finally, proud Bertie was a **confident**, young prince.
In fact, he changed so much that he hasn't stopped talking since!